Dear Parent:

MOOSEHEART SCHOOL
ELEMENTARY LIBRARY

W9-ARH-617

Congratulations! Your child is taking
the first steps on an exciting journey.
The destination? Independent reading!

STEP INTO READING® will help your child get there. The program offers
books at five levels that accompany children from their first attempts at
reading to reading success. Each step includes fun stories, fiction and
nonfiction, and colorful art. There are also Step into Reading Sticker Books,
Step into Reading Math Readers, Step into Reading Write-In Readers, Step into
Reading Phonics Readers, and Step into Reading Phonics First Steps! Boxed
Sets—a complete literacy program with something to interest every child.

Learning to Read, Step by Step!

Ready to Read   Preschool–Kindergarten
• big type and easy words • rhyme and rhythm • picture clues
For children who know the alphabet and are eager to
begin reading.

Reading with Help   Preschool–Grade 1
• basic vocabulary • short sentences • simple stories
For children who recognize familiar words and sound out
new words with help.

Reading on Your Own   Grades 1–3
• engaging characters • easy-to-follow plots • popular topics
For children who are ready to read on their own.

Reading Paragraphs   Grades 2–3
• challenging vocabulary • short paragraphs • exciting stories
For newly independent readers who read simple sentences
with confidence.

Ready for Chapters   Grades 2–4
• chapters • longer paragraphs • full-color art
For children who want to take the plunge into chapter books
but still like colorful pictures.

STEP INTO READING® is designed to give every child a successful
reading experience. The grade levels are only guides. Children can progress
through the steps at their own speed, developing confidence in their
reading, no matter what their grade.

Remember, a lifetime love of reading starts with a single step!

Cover photography by Joe Dias, Jeff O'Brien, Jennifer Hoon, Greg Roccia, David Chickering, and Judy Tsuno

BARBIE and associated trademarks and trade dress are owned by, and used under license from, Mattel, Inc. Copyright © 2004 Mattel, Inc. All Rights Reserved. Published in the United States by Random House Children's Books, a division of Random House, Inc., New York, and simultaneously in Canada by Random House of Canada Limited, Toronto. No part of this book may be reproduced or copied in any form without permission from the copyright owner.

www.stepintoreading.com

www.barbie.com

Educators and librarians, for a variety of teaching tools, visit us at
www.randomhouse.com/teachers

Library of Congress Cataloging-in-Publication Data
Jordan, Apple.
School days / by Apple Jordan ; illustrated by Karen Wolcott. — 1st ed.
    p.   cm. — (Step into reading. A step 1 book) "Barbie."
SUMMARY: Barbie helps Stacie and Kelly get ready for school and then teaches a class herself.
ISBN 0-375-82723-4 (trade) — ISBN 0-375-92723-9 (lib. bdg.)
[1. Morning—Fiction.   2. Schools—Fiction.   3. Dolls—Fiction.]
I. Karen Wolcott, ill.   II. Title.   III. Series: Step into reading. Step 1 book.
PZ7.J755Sc   2004   [E]—dc21   2003008529

Printed in the United States of America   First Edition   10 9 8 7 6 5 4 3 2 1

STEP INTO READING, RANDOM HOUSE, and the Random House colophon are registered trademarks of Random House, Inc.

Barbie™
School Days

by Apple Jordan

illustrated by Karen Wolcott

Random House 🏠 New York

Time for school!
The clock is ringing.

The sun is up.

The birds are singing.

Stacie has a test today.

Kelly cannot
wait to play.

But first they have
so much to do.
They brush their teeth.
They wash up, too.

They make their beds.

They brush their hair.

Then they pick out
what to wear!

Barbie cooks eggs
for Stacie and Kelly.

For lunch they make
peanut butter and jelly.

They pack their bags
with things they need—
pens to write with
and books to read.

SPELLING

They button their coats.

They are on their way.

Everyone is ready for
a new school day!

The school bell rings.

They are not late.

"Good luck, Stacie.
You will do great!"

"So long, Kelly!
Go have fun.
See you when
the day is done."

MOOSEHEART SCHOOL
ELEMENTARY LIBRARY

Barbie rushes.

Hurry! Zoom!

Just on time

to her own classroom!